Nate the Great
Goes Down in
The Dumps

Nate the Great
Goes Down in
The Dumps

by Marjorie Weinman Sharmat
illustrated by Marc Simont

A Yearling Book

For my dog, Fritz Melvin,
who came into my life
when Sludge came into Nate's

Published by
Bantam Doubleday Dell Books for Young Readers
a division of
Bantam Doubleday Dell Publishing Group, Inc.
1540 Broadway
New York, New York 10036

ISBN: 0-440-40438-X

Reprinted by arrangement with The Putnam & Grosset Group on behalf
of Coward-McCann

Printed in the United States of America

April 1991

30 29 28 27 26 25 24

UPR

Nate the Great
Goes Down in The Dumps

I, Nate the Great,
and my dog, Sludge,
were taking a walk.
We walked too far.
We walked to Rosamond's house.
Rosamond and her four cats were
sitting on a crate
behind a table
in front of her house.

There was a crystal ball
on the table.
There was a sign
next to the crystal ball.

"I will read your future,"
Rosamond said. "For two cents."
"My future is worth more
than two cents," I said.
"Three cents then," Rosamond said.

She gazed into her crystal ball.

"You will have a new case to solve
very soon. Three cents."

"I, Nate the Great, always have cases
to solve," I said.

Rosamond gazed into
her crystal ball again.

"I can tell you more," she said.

"Someone has lost a box, a money box.
You have to look for it."

"A money box?" I said.

"How much money is in it?"

"No money," Rosamond said.

"It's empty."

"Empty?"

"Yes. It's my box.

I was going to use it

to hold the money I got

for reading the future."

Sludge was tugging at me to leave.

He did not see any money

in Rosamond's future.

"Don't go," Rosamond said.

"Listen to what happened.

Claude helped me set up my business.

We brought out the table,

this sign, the box,

and four cans of tuna fish

for my cats.

Cats want to know

what's in their future, too.

Like tuna fish."

"Of course," I said.

"I put the sign on the table,"
Rosamond said.

"I put the box on the grass
near the table.

I put the tuna-fish cans
in a neat pile near the box."

"What happened next?" I asked.

"My cats and I went into my house

to get my crystal ball," Rosamond said.
"Claude went into my garage
to get this crate
for my cats and me to sit on.
When I came back with my crystal ball
the crate was here.
The table and the sign
and the tuna-fish cans were still here.
But the cans were tipped over.
The box and Claude were gone."

"When did this happen?" I asked.

"Just before you came along,"
Rosamond said.

"You are my first customer
for reading the future.
Now you have a new case and
you owe me three cents."

"I don't have three cents," I said,
"and you don't have a box
to put it in."

"I will if you solve the case,"
Rosamond said.

"This is a very famous box.

It's the first box that my cat

Super Hex ever slept in."

Rosamond gave me a strange look.

It was the only kind of look she had.

"Very well," I said. "I will take your case.

Does your famous box have a cover?

Does it have a color? What size is it?"

"It's a white box with ROSAMOND

printed on one side of it," Rosamond said.

"It doesn't have a cover.

It's big enough to hold

one hundred dollars in pennies."

"How big is that?" I asked.

Rosamond pointed to her house.

"The box is smaller than my house,

smaller than my garage,

smaller than this crate,

smaller than—"

"Never mind," I said.

Rosamond shrugged. "I read the future.

I don't measure boxes."

I took out my notebook

and tore off a piece of paper.

I wrote a note to my mother.

Rosamond grabbed my note.

"I will deliver this

while you solve my case."

Rosamond walked off

with her four cats.

Sludge and I sat down on the crate.

Dear Mother,
I am on a case
you wouldn't
believe so I won't
tell you about it
I will be back.
Love
Nate the Great

The crate had a label on it: BANANAS.

"Maybe the box is still here

somewhere," I said.

Sludge and I peered under the table.

The box wasn't there.

17

Suddenly we saw legs. Six legs.
Two belonged to Annie,
and four belonged to her dog Fang.
"Can you read my future?" Annie asked.
"No, but I can read Fang's future.
I, Nate the Great, predict that

some day Fang is going to bite

Sludge and me. Today could be the day."

Sludge and I rushed off.

I called back to Annie.

"Have you seen an empty box

with Rosamond's name on it,

and big enough to hold

one hundred dollars in pennies?"

"No," Annie shouted.

"We have to look for Claude,"

I said to Sludge.

Looking for Claude

would be harder

than looking for the box.

Claude was always getting lost.

We went to Claude's house.

I rang his doorbell.

I knocked on his door.

I peeked through his windows.

Somebody tapped me on the shoulder.

It was Claude.

"Are you looking for me?" he asked.

"I was lost but I found myself."

"Good work," I said.

"I am looking for Rosamond's box.

I think you saw it last."

"I saw it on the grass

just before I went into her garage

to get her crate," Claude said.

"Carrying that crate was hard work!

It kept bumping into my stomach.

I put it down on the grass by the table,

just where Rosamond wanted it.

All the time I kept watching

for Rosamond.

I hoped she wouldn't

come out

before I could get away."

"Get away?"

"Yes. I was tired of
being Rosamond's moving man.
After I put the crate down,
I started to run."

"Then what?"

"I tripped over the pile

of tuna-fish cans," Claude said.

"I fell down on the grass.

But the box wasn't there.

I would have seen it."

"That explains why the pile of cans

was tipped over," I said. "But

it doesn't explain where the box went.

I, Nate the Great, say that
somebody must have taken it
while you were in the garage
and Rosamond and her cats
were in her house.
But who would want an empty box
with Rosamond's name on it?"
Claude shrugged.
"Somebody extremely desperate
for a box," I said.
Sludge and I rushed to Finley's house.
Finley owns a rat. The rat sleeps
in a big box until he chews it up.
Then Finley gets a new box.
Maybe it was time for a new box
for Finley's rat.

Maybe Finley took Rosamond's box.
I saw Finley outside with his rat.
There was a big chewed-up box
beside the rat with RAT HOUSE
printed on it.

"I am looking for an empty box

big enough to hold

one hundred dollars in pennies,"

I said. "It belongs to Rosamond."

"My box belongs to my rat," Finley said.

"But there are plenty of boxes at the

supermarket. They have the best ones.

If you can't find Rosamond's box there,

go to the dump.

They have the worst ones."

"I will look for the best," I said.

"I, Nate the Great, do not like dumps."

Sludge and I went to the supermarket.

Sludge had to wait outside.

I went inside. I looked for empty boxes.

I saw open boxes and sacks

full of oranges and potatoes.

I saw open crates

full of tomatoes and bananas and carrots.

I saw labels on the boxes and crates.

I remembered that Rosamond's crate
had the label BANANAS on it.
She probably got her crate
at this supermarket.
But that was no help.
I, Nate the Great, did not need
a crate that said BANANAS,
or a box that said ORANGES.
I needed a box that said ROSAMOND.
Suddenly I smelled something.
Pancakes.
A lady was handing out pancake samples.
I took one.
Then I circled around and took another.
The third time around she said,
"No more."

I left the supermarket.

I, Nate the Great, needed more pancakes.

Sludge needed a bone.

We went home.

We ate and thought.

I kept thinking about the empty box.

There was something else empty, too.

My head.

Was I missing a big clue?

I thought back.

An empty box. A table. A sign.

Four cans of tuna fish.

Rosamond saw all these things

before she and her cats went

into her house.

Claude saw them before he went

into Rosamond's garage.

Then the empty box was gone.

Only the empty box.

Why?

Perhaps the table was too heavy

to take. And no one would take

a sign that said

ROSAMOND READS THE FUTURE. 2¢.

But why not take the cans of tuna fish?

Why take an empty box

that isn't worth anything?

I, Nate the Great, suddenly

had the answer!

Because the box isn't worth anything!

Someone must have seen the empty box

and picked it up and thrown it away.

But it had Rosamond's name on it.

Just on one side.

Maybe her name wasn't seen.

"Rosamond's box has probably gone

to the dump by now," I said to Sludge.

"Where the worst boxes go."

Sludge and I hurried to the town dump.

There were mountains of stuff there.

Old, ripped, wrecked, broken,

disgusting things.

Things that nobody wanted.

I did not want them, either.

"We are down in the dumps,"

I said to Sludge.

But then on top of one mountain

of junk I saw something!

A box was sticking out,

and I could see a big *R*

printed on one side of it!

At last! It must be Rosamond's box.

"We have to climb up that mountain
of junk," I said.

Sludge looked at me.

He did not want to do it.

I did not want to do it.

But we did it.

Up, up we climbed.

Over lumpy mattresses
and broken furniture
and old shoes and ugly clothes.

At last we were at the top of the heap.

I grabbed the empty box.

Now I could read the whole name on it.

RAT HOUSE.

It was not Rosamond's box.

It was a chewed-up box

that had once been a home

for Finley's rat.

I was mad.

I was tired.

Sludge was tired.

We sat down.

I put my arm around Sludge

and we sat there

on top of the world.

On top of the world of junk.

I looked down.

Down was *way* down.

I was afraid to stay

and afraid to leave.

But we had to leave.

"Let's go," I said.

Sludge and I started to climb down.

Sludge was scared.

"Don't look down," I said.

Sludge kept his eyes up.

Then I stopped.

That was it!

The answer to my case.

I had given myself the clue I needed!

"I have just solved the case," I said.

"We must go back to Rosamond's hou

I grabbed a lumpy mattress.

Sludge and I slid

the rest of the way down

on the mattress.

We brushed ourselves off.

Then we rushed to Rosamond's house.

She was sitting on the crate

with her cats, waiting for business.

"I delivered your note," she said.

"Did you find my box?"

"Yes," I said.

"So where is it?" she asked.

"You are sitting on it," I said.

"I'm sitting on a crate,

not a box," she said.

Rosamond and her cats stood up.

"See?"

I leaned down and picked up the crate.

And there, under it, was Rosamond's box!

"My box!" Rosamond said.

"It was inside my crate."

"Yes. Claude put the crate over the box,

but he didn't know it."

Rosamond picked up her box.

"Why didn't he know it?" she asked.

"Claude told me he was carrying
the crate near his stomach," I said,
"and he was looking for you
at the same time.

That meant he was looking
above the crate.

But what was happening *below?*
Claude did not know.

Claude did not look *down.*

Claude did not look down
when he put the crate over the box!
Then he started to run.

He fell. He kicked over the cans.
And that's when he noticed that
the box wasn't there.

After *he* had made it disappear."

"That's the last time I'll ask Claude
to help me," Rosamond said.

"Claude will be glad to hear that,"
I said.

Rosamond hugged her box.

"But how did you figure this out?"

"There were many clues," I said,

"but I didn't know it.

You told me that your box

was smaller than your crate.

That was a clue."

Rosamond was squeezing her box.

"Tell me more clues," she said.

"I saw crates in the supermarket,"

I said. "I figured you got your

BANANAS crate there."

"I bought lots and lots of bananas

at the supermarket," Rosamond said,

"until the banana crate was empty.

Then they gave it to me."

"I, Nate the Great, noticed that
all the crates at the supermarket
had an open top. That meant that
your crate must have an open top.
But you kept your crate upside down
to sit on.
The open top was at the bottom.
And it fit right over your box
and hid it."
Rosamond was all excited.
She was crushing her famous box.
I had done all my hard work
for a crushed box.
But my work was over.
I said, "I solved the case
when Sludge and I were at the dump

and I told him not to look down.

Not looking down was the key clue."

"You went to the dump for me!"

Rosamond exclaimed.

"I must do something for you.

I will read your future

two times for free. Three times.

Ten times. I will give you

as many futures

as you want."

"I can read my own future," I said.

I gazed into the crystal ball.

"I see a detective and his dog," I said.

"They are going to disappear."

And that's what Sludge and I did.